Really, Really

To my really really brave friend Paul d'Auria
K.G.
For Jon
N.S.

REALLY, REALLY
A RED FOX BOOK 978 0 099 41394 3

First published in Great Britain by The Bodley Head,
an imprint of Random House Children's Books

The Bodley Head edition published 2002
Red Fox edition published 2003

9 10 8

Red Fox Books are published by Random House Children's Books,
61-63 Uxbridge Road, London W5 5SA,
a division of The Random House Group Ltd,
Addresses for companies within The Random House Group Limited
can be found at : www.randomhouse.co.uk/offices.htm

THE RANDOM HOUSE GROUP Limited Reg. No. 954009

www.kidsatrandomhouse.co.uk

A CIP catalogue record for this book is available from the British Library.

Printed and bound in Singapore

Really, Really

Kes Gray & Nick Sharratt

RED FOX

Daisy was very excited.
She'd never had a babysitter before.

Daisy's *mum* was very late.
"Daisy meet Angela, Angela meet Daisy!" said Daisy's *mum*,
kissing Daisy on the forehead and then running down
the path to the taxi waiting outside.

Angela the babysitter closed the front door and smiled at Daisy. "Why are you eating paper?" she asked.

"I'm not eating paper," said Daisy.
"Really?" said Angela.
"Really, really," fibbed Daisy.

"You must be hungry," said Angela.
"What do you usually have
for tea?"
"Ice-cream and chips," said Daisy.
"Really?" said Angela.
"Really, really," fibbed Daisy.

"Have you ever had a babysitter before?" asked Angela.

"Hundreds!" said Daisy.

"Really?" said Angela.

"Really, really," fibbed Daisy.

"Would you like a glass of milk?" asked Angela.

"I'm only allowed lemonade," said Daisy.

"Really?" said Angela.

"Really, really," fibbed Daisy.

"What time do you usually go to bed?" asked Angela.
"Midnight at the earliest," said Daisy.
"Really?" said Angela.
"Really, really," fibbed Daisy.

"Do you need to have a bath?" asked Angela.
"I don't get dirty," said Daisy.
"Really?" said Angela.
"Really, really," fibbed Daisy.

"What time do you put your pyjamas on?" asked Angela.
"I always sleep in my clothes," said Daisy.
"Really?" said Angela.
"Really, really," fibbed Daisy.

"Shall we sit down and do some reading?" asked Angela.

"My mum prefers it if I play games," said Daisy.

"What sort of games?" asked Angela.

"Bouncing on the settee and sliding on the table," said Daisy, "until ten o'clock."

"Really?" said Angela.

"Really, really," fibbed Daisy.

"Then we watch videos till midnight," said Daisy.

"Really?" said Angela.

"Really, really," fibbed Daisy.

At midnight Daisy heard a taxi pull up outside her house.
"I'm feeling very sleepy all of a sudden," said Daisy,
jumping off the sofa and scooting upstairs to bed.

Angela opened the front door and Daisy's *mum* tiptoed in.

"Hello Angela," whispered Daisy's *mum*.

"Has Daisy been a good girl? She did give you my note didn't she? She did have a proper tea didn't she? She did have a bath and wash her hair? She did put clean pyjamas on didn't she? She was in bed by eight wasn't she? And she didn't charge around the house like a mad thing did she?"

Angela put her hands behind her back and crossed her fingers.

"She's been as good as gold," said Angela. "She's been a little angel."

"Really?" asked Daisy's *mum*.

"Really, really," fibbed Angela.

What will Daisy do next?!

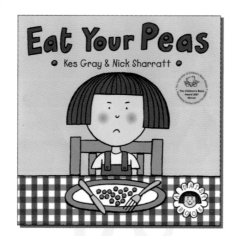

Now with a fantastic pull-out and play frieze and 40 stickers so you can act out Daisy's adventures!

A new longer Daisy story book!

Come and play with Daisy at www.daisyclub.co.uk